In memory of Frances Lincoln – A.S.
For my father, with love – L.C.

First published in Great Britain in 2002 by
Frances Lincoln Limited, 4 Torriano Mews
Torriano Avenue, London NW5 2RZ

www.franceslincoln.com

British Library Cataloguing in Publication Data
available on request

ISBN 0-7112-1884-6

Set in Myriad Regular

Printed in Singapore
1 3 5 7 9 8 6 4 2

DAN'S ANGEL

A Detective's Guide to the Language of Painting

Alexander Sturgis

Illustrated by Lauren Child

FRANCES LINCOLN

Dan wanted to be a detective. He was always
looking for clues with his magnifying glass,
but he was never sure what sort of clues
he was looking for.

One day he was whizzing along on his
skateboard, when he came across a large
building he hadn't seen before.

"There's bound to be a really useful clue
in here," he said, as he pushed open the door.

Inside, Dan gasped with amazement.

The walls were covered with paintings, full of strange and beautiful things. Some seemed to tell stories, but he couldn't work out what the stories were.

"You can't read paintings like you can read books," he sighed.

TICKETS

RESTAURANT
AND
SHOP

"You can read this one," a voice said. It seemed to come from a painting of an angel talking to a woman.

Dan saw words coming out of the angel's mouth, but he couldn't understand them. "Maybe it's code," he thought.

"It's Latin," the voice said. Dan jumped. The angel was talking to him!

"Well, what does it say?" Dan asked, pretending he was used to talking to painted angels.

"I'm telling Mary she's going to have a baby," the angel said proudly. "I'm Gabriel, God's messenger."

The Annunciation,
BY FRA ANGELICO
painted in about 1432.

The moment when the angel Gabriel tells Mary she is going to have a baby is called the Annunciation ('the announcement').

Dan looked at the writing again. "That's odd," he said.
"The middle line's upside down."

"That's what Mary's saying back to me," said Gabriel.
"She's asking me to tell God how happy she is. But I don't
know why the words are upside down."

"Maybe so that they can be read by someone up in heaven," Dan said.

"Why didn't I think of that?" said Gabriel.
"Now, follow me." And with that, he flapped
out of his painting into the gallery.

"This isn't how painted angels should behave," said Dan, hurrying after the angel.

Gabriel stopped beside a big, dark picture. "OK, Mr Detective," he said. "Tell me about this man."

Belshazzar's Feast
BY REMBRANDT, *about 1636-8*.

When the evil king Belshazzar was feasting, a hand wrote a message on the wall telling him his kingdom would be destroyed.

Dan looked for clues. "Well," he said, "he's a king. He likes gold –
and he's terrified. Look! His eyes are popping out of his head.
He's only just seen that strange glowing writing being written
by a floating hand."

"How do you know he's only just seen it?" Gabriel asked.

"Because the wine's still falling out of the cup he's knocked over,"
said Dan. "And no one else has seen the writing yet. They're looking
at the king, thinking he's gone crazy."

"You don't miss much, do you?" said Gabriel. Before Dan could
answer, he had swooped off into the next room.

Perseus and Andromeda
BY PIERO DI COSIMO, *painted in about 1515.*

The Greek hero Perseus rescued the princess Andromeda
from a sea-monster. Afterwards he married her.

Dan found Gabriel flapping excitedly beside a painting. There was an amazing monster in the picture with elephant tusks and a corkscrew tail. But that wasn't why Gabriel was in such a flutter.

"All right, Mr Detective," he said. "I'll give you ride on my back if you can tell me how many people are wearing helmets in this picture. If you're wrong, I get a ride on your skateboard."

There was a man with a helmet and winged shoes waving his sword on top of the monster. Another helmeted man was flying in the sky, and Dan found a third in the crowd on the right.

"But why is Gabriel sure I'll get it wrong?" he wondered. "I know!" he cried. "They're all the same person. First the man's flying in the sky. Then he fights the monster to rescue the woman tied to the tree – and then everyone's dancing and clapping on the right."

"You win," said Gabriel, a bit put out. "Hop on, then." And together they flew off across the room.

Gabriel set Dan down with a bump.

"Tell me about that picture," said Dan. He pointed to a painting of a group of people in a garden. Dan was sure the mother and baby were Mary and Jesus. But who were the others?

"Those are holy men and women, called saints," said Gabriel. "You can tell which saint is which, because each one has their own special symbol."

"So that isn't a pet lamb," Dan said, looking at the man in green.

"No – that's the saint's symbol. He's Saint John the Baptist, and he called Jesus 'the Lamb of God'. Saint Anthony always has a pig, because his followers kept pigs, and Saint Barbara has a tower – she was locked in one by her dad, you know," Gabriel added.

"Who's that with the book and sword?" asked Dan.

"That," said Gabriel, "is Saint Catherine, and her most important symbol is almost covered by her dress. It's –"

". . . a Catherine wheel!" cried Dan.

Madonna and Child with Saints
BY A FOLLOWER OF ROBERT CAMPION
painted in the 1440s or 1450s.

Mary and Jesus sit in front of a cloth woven with
gold and have striped golden halos around their heads.

Round the corner was a beautifully-painted country scene with goats and sheep and a group of strange people.

"That little boy has wings. Is he an angel?" asked Dan.

"Certainly not," said Gabriel. "He's a Roman god, and those women are goddesses."

Dan noticed a peacock behind a goddess. "Maybe the peacock's a symbol," he said. "Will it tell us who the goddess is?"

"Yes." said Gabriel. "She's Juno, queen of the gods. Her chariot was always pulled by peacocks. And Minerva, the warrior-goddess of wisdom, always has a helmet."

"And I bet the winged boy belongs to the goddess with no clothes on," said Dan.

"You've got it," said Gabriel. "She's Venus, goddess of love, and the boy is her son Cupid. He fires arrows at people's hearts to make them fall in love."

Gabriel glided off into the next room, and Dan chased after him.

The Judgement of Paris
BY CLAUDE LORRAIN, *painted in about 1645.*
The shepherd Paris had to judge who was the most beautiful goddess. He chose Venus and gave her the prize of a golden apple.

Dan found Gabriel peering at an amazing picture of a woman with lots of arms, standing on top of a big black animal.

"I think it's a buffalo," said Gabriel. "But what's happened to its head?"

"Yuk!" said Dan. "The tiger's having it for lunch. I think the devil was hiding inside the buffalo."

"He doesn't look too happy," said Gabriel.

"That's because he's lost the fight," said Dan. "Look, his sword's broken and that woman's pulling him out of the buffalo with a red rope."

"She's a very strange woman," said Gabriel.

"I can see that," said Dan. "She's got eighteen arms."

"Why do you think she's got so many?" asked Gabriel.

"Is it because she's so powerful?" suggested Dan. "Maybe each hand is holding a different symbol of her power – some are weapons, but she has some peaceful symbols as well. You can't fight with a flower, can you?"

"You're right," said Gabriel. "She's a really powerful Indian goddess called Durga."

***Devi Battles
the Buffalo Demon Mahisha***
By an artist from the
Kingdom of Chamba,
Punjab Hills, India
painted in about 1830
When the goddess Durga defeated
the demon Mahisha, all the other gods
and goddesses celebrated up in the clouds.

Just then, a little dog wearing a ribbon round its neck started yapping at Dan's feet.

"What a funny dog," thought Dan, as it trotted off and jumped into a painting of a woman wearing a ribbon round her very, very thin waist. "It must be her pet."

"Yes, it is," said Gabriel flapping up behind him, "but dogs can be symbols too – symbols of faithfulness."

Dan wondered why such a smartly-dressed woman had a symbol of faithfulness beside her. Then he noticed all the flowers. There were roses in her dress and she was holding a big pink carnation.

"You give flowers to someone you love, so maybe flowers are symbols of love," he said. "And a dog means she will always be faithful to her loved one."

"You really *are* a detective," said Gabriel. "This portrait was painted for the lady's husband when they got married."

The Marquesa de Pontejos
BY FRANCISCO DE GOYA,
probably painted in 1786.

The Marquesa was a very rich,
24-year-old Spanish woman. When
she was painted, it was fashionable
for young women to have grey hair.

Soap Bubbles
By Jean-Siméon Chardin,
probably painted in 1733-4.

The glass beside the boy
is full of soapy water.

"Can anything be a symbol?" asked Dan, as they made their way into the next room.

"Well, lots of things can," answered Gabriel. "Bubbles, for instance." They stopped in front of a painting of a boy blowing a big bubble out of a straw. Behind him, a younger boy was trying to get a better look.

"What are bubbles symbols of?" asked Dan.

"You tell me," said Gabriel. "You're the detective."

"Well," said Dan, "you can't catch bubbles. They don't last very long. And they pop."

"So a bubble is a bit like childhood," said Gabriel. "You can't hold on to it – you can't stay young for ever."

"Perhaps the painting is saying: don't waste your childhood blowing bubbles, because before you know it, you'll grow up and pop!" suggested Dan.

"I couldn't have put it better myself!" laughed Gabriel. "Here – follow me, Mr Detective."

Venus and Mars
BY SANDRO BOTTICELLI,
painted around 1485.

This painting may once
have been part of a piece
of furniture – perhaps a bed.

Gabriel swooped into the next room and hovered beside a painting
of a man and a woman lying on the grass.

Dan looked at the children. "What hairy legs!" he said.
"And they've got horns."

"Those are fauns," said Gabriel. "They're half-man and half-goat."

"Who are the man and woman?" asked Dan.

"The woman is Venus, the goddess of love, again," said Gabriel.
"Cupid's not with her this time. Can you work out who the man is?"

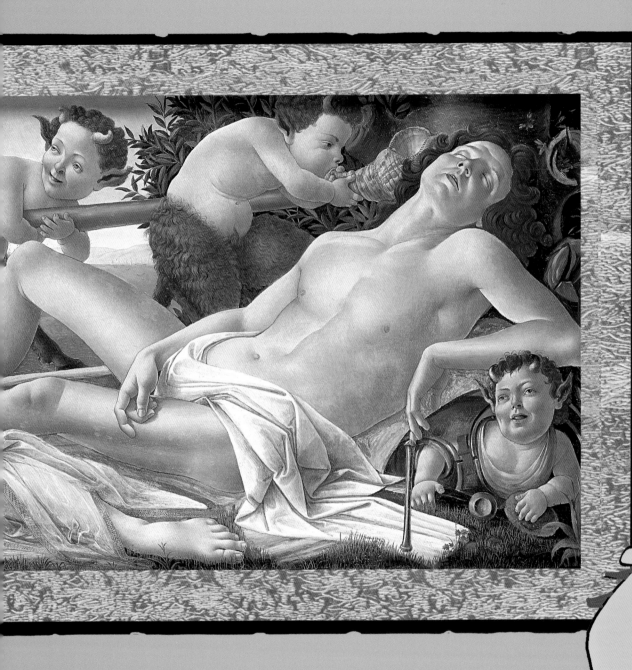

Dan looked at the armour and weapons around the sleeping man. "Maybe he's the god of war," he said. "But he doesn't look very war-like. He's taken off his armour and he's exhausted. Even the faun blowing a shell into his ear can't wake him up."

"He's fast asleep," said Gabriel, with a little flap. "But Venus isn't, is she?"

"I see…" said Dan. "So love is more powerful than war."

"And that's the message of the painting," said Gabriel. "It's easy when you know how."

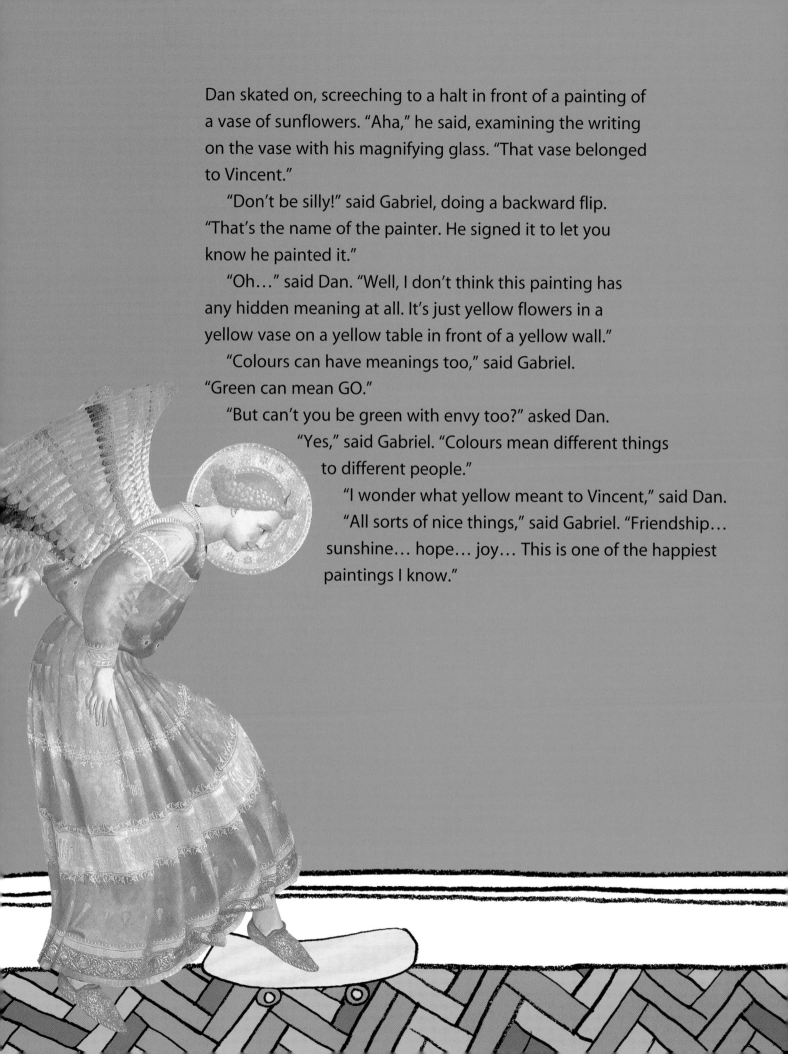

Dan skated on, screeching to a halt in front of a painting of a vase of sunflowers. "Aha," he said, examining the writing on the vase with his magnifying glass. "That vase belonged to Vincent."

"Don't be silly!" said Gabriel, doing a backward flip. "That's the name of the painter. He signed it to let you know he painted it."

"Oh…" said Dan. "Well, I don't think this painting has any hidden meaning at all. It's just yellow flowers in a yellow vase on a yellow table in front of a yellow wall."

"Colours can have meanings too," said Gabriel. "Green can mean GO."

"But can't you be green with envy too?" asked Dan.

"Yes," said Gabriel. "Colours mean different things to different people."

"I wonder what yellow meant to Vincent," said Dan.

"All sorts of nice things," said Gabriel. "Friendship… sunshine… hope… joy… This is one of the happiest paintings I know."

Sunflowers
By Vincent van Gogh,
painted in 1888.

Van Gogh painted four pictures
of sunflowers to decorate the bedroom
of his friend, the artist Paul Gauguin.
This is one of them.

Weeping Woman
By PABLO PICASSO,
painted in 1937.

The woman may be weeping over
a dead loved one. The Spanish Picasso
painted several pictures of weeping
women after the outbreak
of a civil war in Spain.

Before Dan knew it, Gabriel was calling him over to
another painting.

Dan could see it was supposed to be a woman's face,
but she was yellow and green! He could make out a mouth,
eyes and ear, but nothing seemed to be in the right place.

"What a mess," Dan said. "People don't look like that."

"Of course they don't," said Gabriel, "but perhaps the artist
wanted to paint what she felt like, not what she looked like."

Dan could see the woman wasn't happy. Her mouth looked
as if she was crying, and the colours made her look ill. Her face
was made up of jagged sharp shapes. Her eyes seemed to
be falling out of their sockets. "She looks all broken up,"
said Dan, "as if she's falling to pieces."

"That's how you feel when you're really sad,"
said Gabriel. "Come on, let's try and find
something to cheer us up."
And he dragged Dan off
into the last room
of the gallery.

Gabriel stopped in front of a huge picture with splashes of black, grey and pink paint all over it.

Dan thought the thin black streaks looked a bit like a spider's web. He felt he was looking through the web into a pinky misty distance.

"Great!" said Dan.

"But it doesn't mean anything," said Gabriel.

"No," said Dan. "When you get close, it looks all splattered and messy, and it feels wild, but when you step back, it looks calm and smooth like a polished stone. And," he said, getting out his magnifying glass, "I think I'll be able to find who painted it."

"I'll tell you who painted it," laughed Gabriel. "His name's at the bottom."

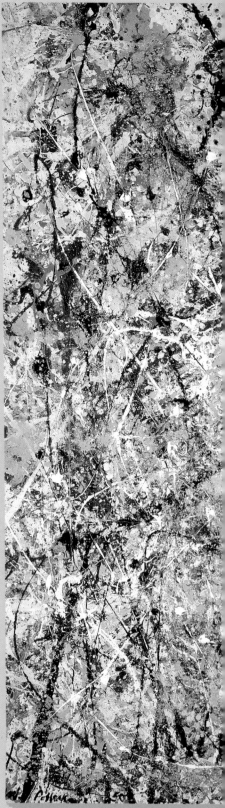

***Number 1, 1950
(Lavender Mist)***
By Jackson Pollock,
painted in 1950.

Jackson Pollock made his pictures
by dripping, pouring and throwing
paint on to the canvas when it
was flat on the floor.

Suddenly Gabriel's expression changed. "Oh, no!" he shrieked, flapping wildly. "I think they're after me."

A red-faced museum guard burst into the room. "One of our angels is missing," he panted. "Have you seen him?"

Dan looked around – but Gabriel had vanished.

"He's always doing this," muttered the guard. "Just wait until I catch him!"

Dan followed the guard out. Through an archway he caught a glimpse of Gabriel's picture. The angel was back in place, giving his message to Mary.

But as Dan walked out through the revolving doors, he looked back – and Gabriel gave him a little wave.

p23 **The Marquesa
de Pontejos** *(c.1786)*
FRANCISCO DE GOYA *(1746–1828)*
National Gallery of Art, Washington
(Andrew W. Mellon Collection)

p24 **Soap Bubbles**
(probably 1733–4)
JEAN-SIMÉON CHARDIN
(1699–1779)
National Gallery of Art, Washington
(Gift of Mrs John W. Simpson)

pp26-27 **Venus and Mars** *(about 1485)*
SANDRO BOTTICELLI *(about 1445–1510)*
The National Gallery, London

p29 **Sunflowers** *(1888)*
VINCENT VAN GOGH *(1853–1890)*
The National Gallery, London

p30 **Weeping Woman** *(1937)*
PABLO PICASSO *(1881–1973)*
Tate Gallery, London

pp32-33 **Number 1, 1950 (Lavender Mist)**
JACKSON POLLOCK *(1912–1956)*
National Gallery of Art, Washington
(Ailsa Mellon Bruce Fund)

PHOTOGRAPHIC ACKNOWLEDGEMENTS

For permission to reproduce the paintings on the following
pages and for supplying photographs, the Publishers would
like to thank:

The National Gallery of Art, Washington © 2002 Board of
Trustees: 17, 18-19, 23, 24, 32-33 (© ARS, NY & DACS,
London 2002)
The National Gallery, London: 12, 26-27, 29
Scala, Florence: 10, 11, 14-15
© Tate, London 2002: 30 (© Succession Picasso/DACS 2002)
V&A Picture Library: 21